TROUBLE ON THE T-BALL TEAM

TROUBLE ON THE T-BALL TEAM

BY EVE BUNTING
ILLUSTRATED BY IRENE TRIVAS

Clarion Books/New York

Clarion Books
a Houghton Mifflin Company imprint
215 Park Avenue South, New York, NY 10003
Text copyright © 1997 by Eve Bunting
Illustrations copyright © 1997 by Irene Trivas

The illustrations for this book were executed in watercolor.
The text was set in 13/17-point Century Old Style.

For information about this and other Houghton Mifflin trade and reference
books and multimedia products, visit The Bookstore at Houghton Mifflin on the
World Wide Web at (http://www.hmco.com/trade/).

Printed in Singapore

Library of Congress Cataloging-in-Publication Data

Bunting, Eve, 1928–
Trouble on the T-ball team / by Eve Bunting ; illustrated by Irene Trivas.
p.   cm.
Summary: Linda feels left out as the only one on her first-grade
T-ball team who hasn't "lost one."
ISBN 0-395-66060-2
[1. T-ball—Fiction   2. Teeth—Fiction.]   I. Trivas, Irene, ill.
II. Title.
PZ7.B91527Ts   1996
[E]—dc20   94-43699
CIP
AC
TWP   10 9 8 7 6 5 4 3 2 1

Our T-ball team is called the Dodgers.
There are ten players. Some of us are boys and some of us are girls.
But something mysterious is happening.
We are losing things. And I don't mean T-ball games.

Jennifer Crow lost one on the way to the game.
Her mom was driving and they had to stop.

"How awful!" we said.
"Did your mom cry?" Brody Broski asked. "My grandma did."

"Don't worry about it now," Coach Sloan said. "Play ball!"
So we did. And I caught a pop fly.
But I was still worried.

I guess you're not safe anywhere.

Abby Pevas lost one at Burger Queen. She was really upset. She said she couldn't finish her hamburger.

"I could *always* finish my hamburger," Brody Broski said.

I'm sure.

If I lost one, I'd be like Abby. I wouldn't finish my hamburger. Or my French fries either.

Carol and Tom Wu are twins.
They both lost one on the same day.
"Twins are funny that way," Tom said.
"Twins are funny that way," Carol said.
"Sometimes we lose things at the same time," Carol said.
"Sometimes we lose things at the same time," Tom said.

That *is* funny.
But poor Manny García lost two at the same time.
And there's only one of him.
How super awful!

Today, Susan Jackson was playing second base.
She missed Brody Broski's throw.
A big, yellow dog was chasing a Frisbee. Susan was watching him.
He caught the Frisbee in his mouth.

Brody Broski was mad. He said the dog could catch better than
Susan. He said she should catch the ball in her mouth.

Brody Broski is mean.

Susan looked worried.

"Don't listen to him," I said.

"I'm not," Susan said. She grinned at me. "I just lost one."

Worst of all was what happened to Karen Connor.
She lost one.
She found it in her aunt's purse.
"I went to look for candy and there it was!" Karen said.
Karen said it was a shock.

We were shocked, too.
"Your very own aunt took it?" Carol Wu asked.
"Your very own aunt?" Tom Wu asked.
Who can a person trust?

Today, D.K. Wood started hopping up and down.
It was the third inning.
"Time out for a bathroom break," Coach Sloan called.

We tossed the ball around.

The big yellow dog came and joined in. Abby Pevas put her Dodger cap on him. He looked so cute.

Susan and I never throw to Brody Broski. He is not our friend.

D.K. began yelling as he ran back. "I lost one in the bathroom."

We gasped. "In the bathroom?"

Coach Sloan patted D.K.'s shoulder. "I lost twenty when I was your age. I haven't lost one since."

We gasped again. "Twenty! How gross!"

Poor Coach Sloan.

After the game today we stood around. We had juice and apple slices. I felt strange. I'm the only Dodger who hasn't lost one. I can't help it. I feel left out.

"You'll be next, sweetie," Dad says. "I can tell."

Dad's mostly right.

I hope so. I didn't think I wanted to lose one. But now I do.

I don't want to be the only strange Dodger on the team. And there's only one game left.

It's the last game. It's the last inning. We're playing the Pirates.
The ball is on the T.
I'm up to bat. I hit it to first base.

The Pirate drops it.
I'm running.
She picks it up
and throws to second.
I'm still running.
The Pirate on second
overthrows to third.

I'm running hard.

The Pirate on third is chasing the ball. So is the big yellow dog. Whose side is he on, anyway?

Everyone's yelling, "Go away, dog! Scat!"

I run for home base. The yellow dog is running beside me. He's a Dodger again. We're steaming!

I look around to see who has the ball. The third baseman is throwing for home. He's a mile off. I'm going to make it. I do. And then I fall over the big yellow dog.

Everyone's calling, "Are you all right, Linda?"

Coach Sloan comes and dusts off my white pants. "Home run, Linda. Way to go! Are you OK?"

I'm OK. But something has happened. I know it. I feel it. Yippee!

Brody Broski rushes from the dugout. He gives me a high-
five. Brody's not so bad. All the Dodgers come out.
They high-five me. They high-five the big yellow dog.

I'm so excited I can hardly stand it. At last . . . I've lost one. I open my other hand and look down at it. It's beautiful!

The big yellow dog and I run to the stands.
Mom and Dad are in the front row.
I grin at them.

"Linda! You've lost your very first tooth," Mom says. She sounds as if she might cry. Like Brody Broski's grandma.

I hold the tooth out in my hand. "Here, Mom. You can put it in your purse. That's what Karen Connor's aunt did."

"I guess the tooth fairy will be coming to our house tonight," Dad says.

Dad's mostly right, so I'm sure she will.

I suck at the space where my tooth used to be. It's on top, in front. The space feels great. I'll be able to whistle "America the Beautiful" through it. That's what Susan does.

It's so good to be a real part of the team . . . at last.